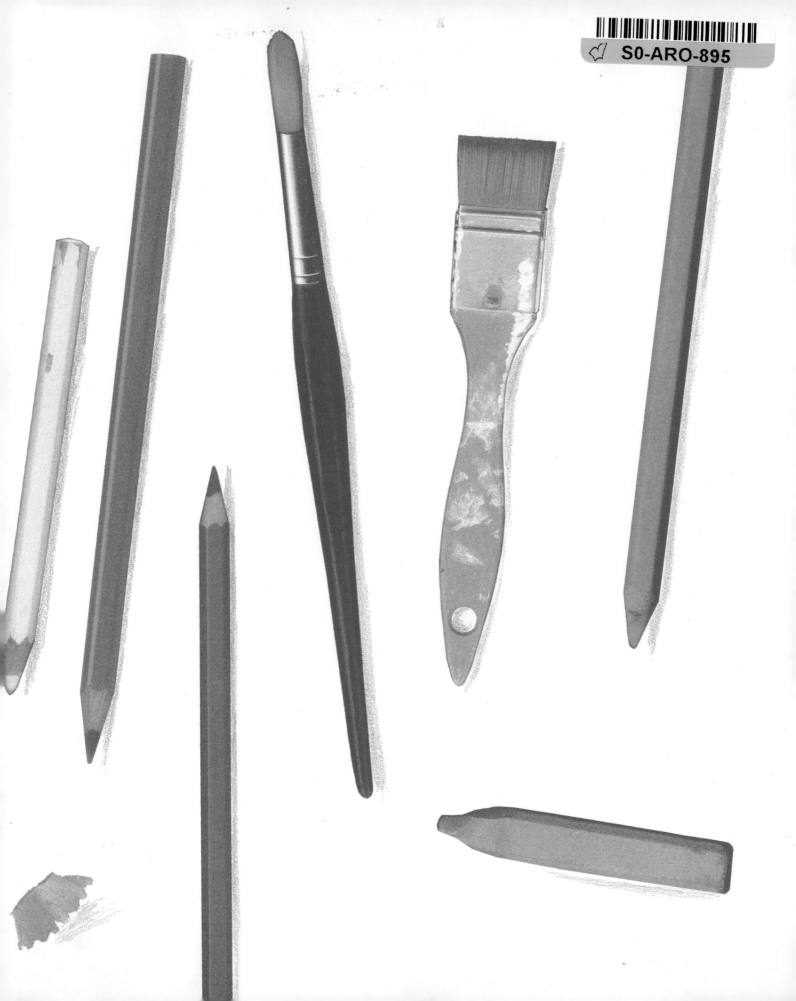

DOG LOVES DRAWING

LOUISE YATES

ALFRED A. KNOPF
New York

Dog loved books!
He loved books
so much that he
opened
his own
bookshop.

When he wasn't
sharing books with
others, Dog was
reading them
himself.

One morning, a package arrived.

Inside was a book,
but as Dog opened
it up, he saw to
his surprise that
it had no words
and no pictures!
"How curious,"
he thought.

Just inside the cover, he noticed a message
from his Aunt Dora that read:

To my dearest Dog,
May the lines you draw open
a door to some wonderful
adventures. With Love from your
Aunt Dora
x x x x

It was a sketchbook!

Dog knew exactly
what to do.

He pulled out his pens, laid out his brushes,

sharpened

his

pencils,

took a deep breath and drew a   door.

He stepped through it,
and on the empty
page in front of him,
Dog drew a stickman.

"Hello," said
the stickman.

"Hello," said Dog.

"I'm not sure what else to draw."

"Let's DOODLE!" suggested the stickman. "That's the best way to come up with ideas." So that is what they did.

Then they turned the page together.

"It would be even more fun
if there were others to join in!"
said Dog. So Dog
drew a duck,

and the duck
drew an owl,
and the owl
drew a crab,
and the crab

did some
coloring in.

Soon they were all
spilling onto the . . .

. . . next page.

"What now?" they wondered.

uck duck duck duck

"Let's go on an outing!"
hooted the owl.

So Dog drew a train

and they all climbed aboard.

While the duck was arguing with the
others about who should drive,
the stickman drew himself a driver's hat,

scribbled
some steam,
and . . .

. . . they were off!

The scenery
streaked
past them—
they were
traveling so
FAST!

At last, the stickman drew
the train to a stop.

Dog got out and drew a boat

while
the crab
scribbled
some sea.

They climbed aboard
(all except the crab, who clung on to the side).

The stickman drew some sandwiches
because he was very hungry.

The owl copied the sandwiches
because she was hungry too,

and the duck drew an enormous cake
because he was the hungriest
of them all!

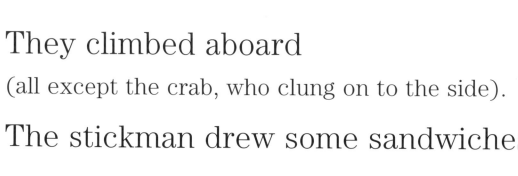

Dog colored in a
cloudless sky and
they drifted. . . .

The boat drifted a long way

before land appeared.

They all got out and stretched their legs.

The crab drew a parasol to protect himself from the sun.

Then the duck decided to draw a . . .

...MONSTER!

And that

spoiled everything.

The monster chased them
all the way round the island
and onto the . . .

. . . next page.

Then Dog had a brilliant idea.

He quickly drew a door

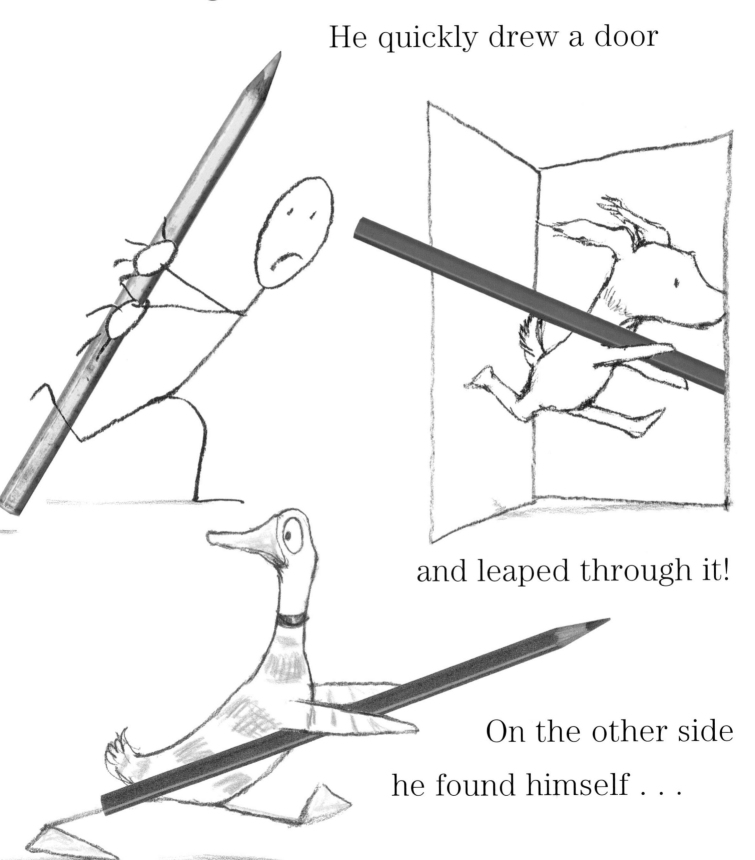

and leaped through it!

On the other side

he found himself . . .

. . . back in
the bookshop!

He turned to the last page of his sketchbook and made sure that all his friends were safe and that the monster could not escape.

Then he dashed out to
buy some more paper.

Dog loves drawing!

And the very next thing he drew was a thank-you card for his Aunt Dora.

ear Aunt Dora,
hank you very
much for my
sketchbook.
with Love from
DOG xxx

For those who taught and encouraged me to draw

THIS IS A BORZOI BOOK PUBLISHED BY ALFRED A. KNOPF

Visit us on the Web! randomhouse.com/kids

Educators and librarians, for a variety of teaching tools, visit us at randomhouse.com/teachers

Library of Congress Cataloging-in-Publication Data
Yates, Louise.
Dog loves drawing / Louise Yates. — 1st American ed.
p.   cm.
Summary: Dog loves drawing so much that he draws his very own adventure.
ISBN 978-0-375-87067-5 (trade) — ISBN 978-0-375-97067-2 (lib. bdg.)
[1. Drawing—Fiction. 2. Dogs—Fiction. 3. Animals—Fiction.] I. Title.
PZ7.Y276Dog 2012
[E]—dc23
2011032353

The illustrations in this book were created using pencil and watercolor.

MANUFACTURED IN MALAYSIA
August 2012
10 9 8 7 6 5 4 3 2 1

First American Edition